NEW HAVEN FREE PUBLIC LIBRARY
W9-BAI-022

DATE DUE

MAR 22 2001
MAY 24 2001
JUL 30 2001
AUG 24 2001
SEP 11 2001
DEC 15 2001
DEC 31 2001
FEB 02 2002
FEB 10 2002
APR 1 2002
MAR 01 2002
NOV 13 2002
DEC 17 2002
MAR 05 2003
MAR 5 04
JUL 21 2003
SEP - 4 2003
FEB 28 2004
APR 10 2010
JUN 27 2014
MAY 30 2006
APR 26 2008
SEP 11 2012
NOV 01 2012
OCT 01 2013
APR 03 2014
FEB 06 2010
DEC 11 2012
JUL 24 2014

NEW HAVEN FREE PUBLIC LIBRARY
133 ELM STREET
NEW HAVEN, CT 06510

Run • Jump • Whiz • Splash

VERA ROSENBERRY

HOLIDAY HOUSE / NEW YORK

Copyright © 1999 by Vera Rosenberry
All Rights Reserved
Printed in the United States of America
Book design by Vera Rosenberry & Sylvia Frezzolini Severance
First Edition

Library of Congress Cataloging-in-Publication Data
Rosenberry, Vera.
Run, jump, whiz, splash / by Vera Rosenberry.—lst ed.
p. cm.
Summary: Illustrations and simple text describe some sights and sounds associated with each season.
ISBN 0-8234-1378-0
[1. Seasons—Fiction.] I. Title.
PZ7.R719155Ru 1999
[E]—dc21 98-14060
CIP
AC

CHILDREN'S ROOM

E
ROSEN-
BERRY

For Tanya and Raman

Summer
is when

the milky white moon rises up

And you

barefoot
over cool, dewy grass

Catching lightning bugs in a jar.

Then you let them go.

Autumn
is when

the fluttery pile of dry leaves grows

And you

so high
in the crunch and smell

And sink, sink, sink down,

the sky above.

Then you jump again.

Winter
is when

the mill pond is snowy
and still

And you

on skates

across smooth, silver ice

As swans fly up
from pale dry reeds

And an old goose scolds.

Spring
is when

the rain-filled creek bubbles and laughs

And you

in boots

upstream through dripping woods

While bluebells nod
in a clean, wet breeze

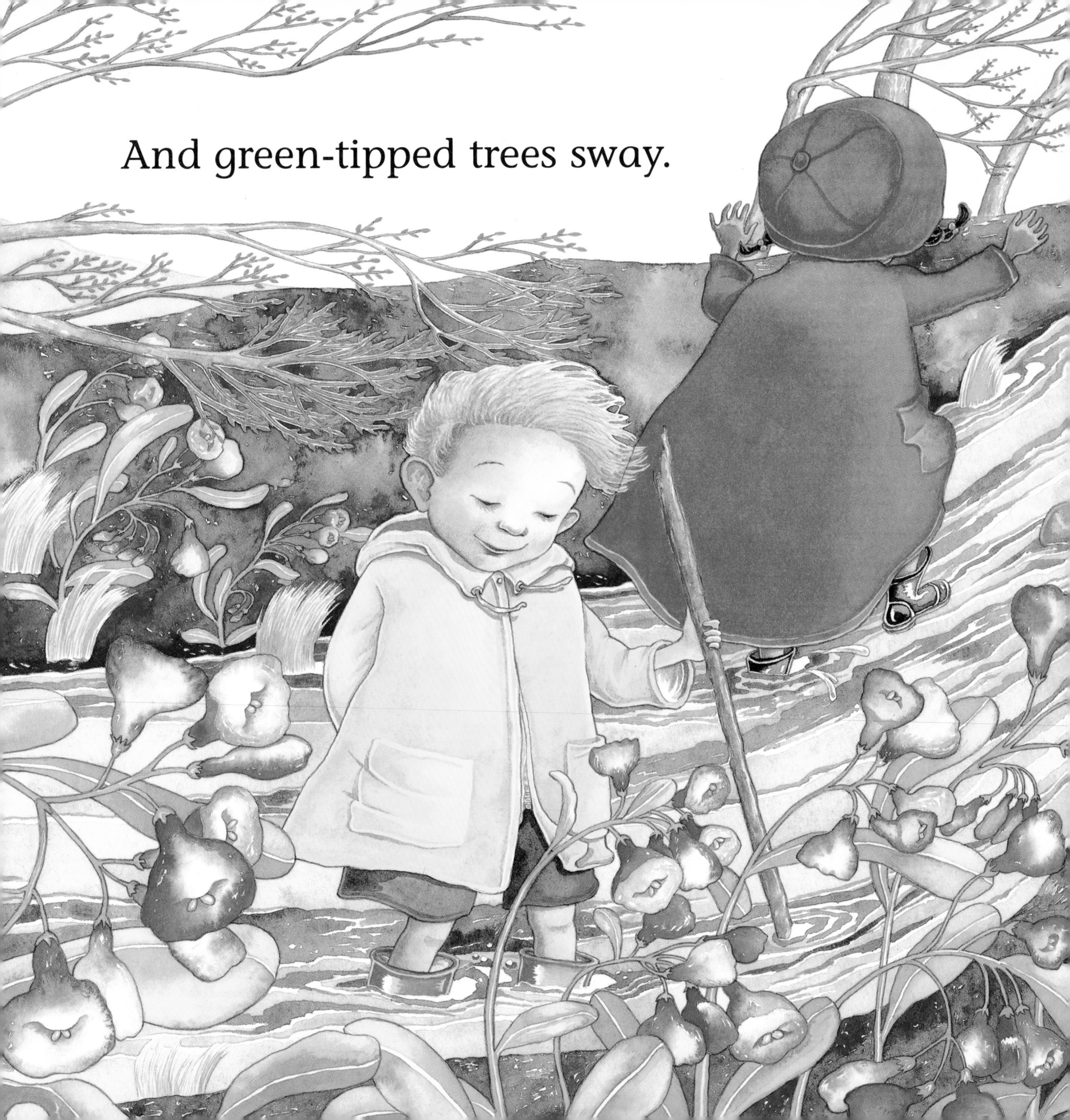

And green-tipped trees sway.

Run

Jump

Whiz

Splash

all the way home.

SEP 2000